Welcoming Elijah

A CROSSOVER TALE WITH A TAIL

Lesléa Newman • illustrated by Susan Gal

ıɛˈı Charlesbridge

For my sweet Passover family:
Barbara, Josee, Hanna, Linda,
Warren, Nathan, and Isabelle—L. N.

For Deborah and Bella—S. G.

Published by Charlesbridge
85 Main Street
Watertown, MA 02472
(617) 926-0329
www.charlesbridge.com

Library of Congress Cataloging-in-Publication Data
Names: Newman, Lesléa, author. | Gal, Susan, illustrator.
Title: Welcoming Elijah : a Passover tale with a tail /
Lesléa Newman ; [illustrations by Susan Gal].
Description: Watertown, MA : Charlesbridge, [2019] |
Summary: Inside the house, a boy prepares for the Passover
ritual of welcoming Elijah—meanwhile outside the house, a
kitten waits in the cold. Identifiers: LCCN 2017060500 |
ISBN 9781580898829 (reinforced for library use) | ISBN
9781632897428 (ebook) | ISBN 9781632897435 (ebook pdf)
Subjects: LCSH: Elijah (Biblical prophet)—Juvenile
fiction. | Passover—Customs and practices—Juvenile
fiction. | Kittens—Juvenile fiction. | CYAC: Elijah
(Biblical prophet)—Fiction. | Passover—Fiction. | Cats—
Fiction. Classification: LCC PZ7.N47988 We 2019 |
DDC [E]—dc23 LC record available at https://lccn.loc.
gov/2017060500

Printed in China
(hc) 10 9 8 7 6 5 4 3 2 1

Illustrations done in ink, charcoal, and digital collage.
Display type set in Blue Liquid by Creativeqube Design
Text type set in Catalina Clemente by Kimmy Design
Color separations by Colourscan Print Co Pte Ltd,
    Singapore
Printed by 1010 Printing International Limited in
    Huizhou, Guangdong, China
Production supervision by Brian G. Walker
Designed by Jacqueline Noelle Cote & Joyce White

032032.1K1/B1483/A4

And that's how Elijah
found a home.

Inside, candles glowed.
Outside, stars twinkled.

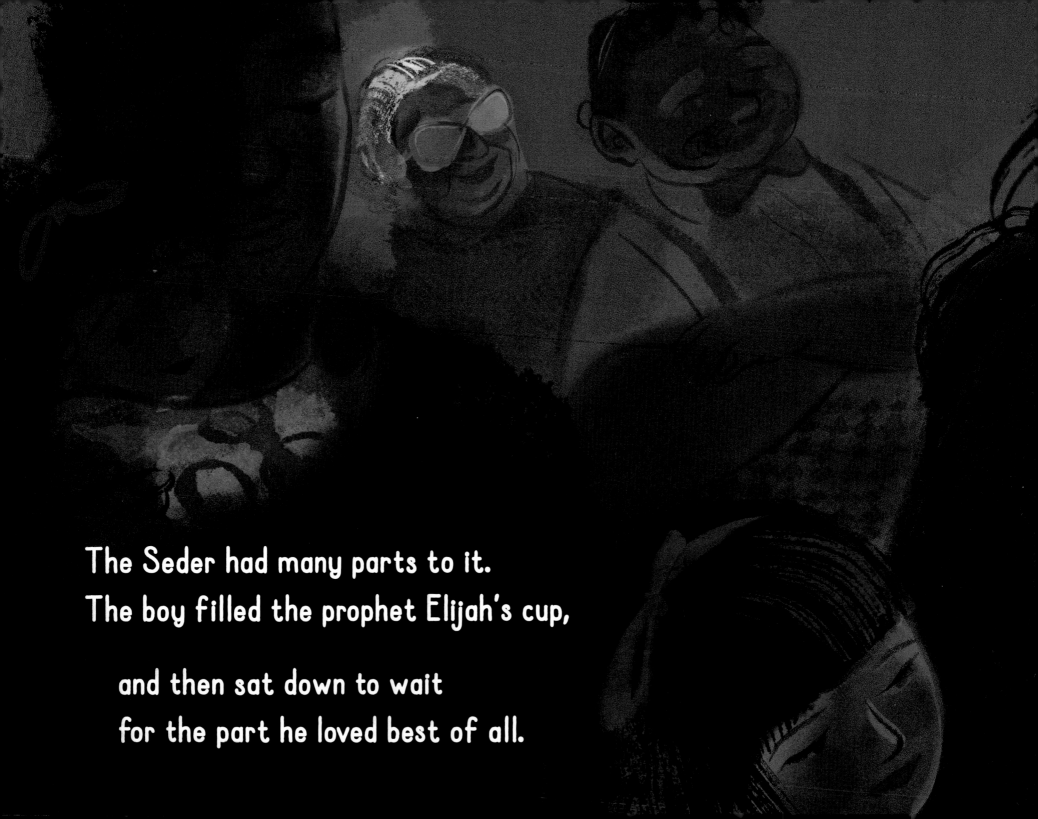

The Seder had many parts to it.
The boy filled the prophet Elijah's cup,

and then sat down to wait
for the part he loved best of all.

Tonight would be different
from all other nights.

The boy knew this.
The kitten did, too.

Inside, the boy waited
for the Seder to start.

Outside, the kitten waited
for the moon to rise.

Inside, a boy hugged his family.
Outside, a kitten sat alone.

Inside, there was laughter.
Outside, there was silence.

Inside, it was warm.
Outside, it was windy.

Inside, there was light.
Outside, there was darkness.

Inside, the boy looked outside.
Outside, the kitten looked inside.

A square of lamplight spilled onto the porch.
A beam of moonlight shone into the hall.

Inside, the boy sprang up from his seat.
Outside, the kitten scampered up the walk.

At last one of the grown-ups said,
"Let us now open the door

to welcome the prophet Elijah
who will one day bring peace to the world."

Still the boy waited.
Still the kitten waited.

Inside, the boy sang songs of praise.
Outside, the kitten mewled.

Inside, the boy patted his full belly.

Outside, the kitten swished its skinny tail.

Inside, the boy ate the festive Passover meal.

Outside, the kitten ate nothing at all.

Outside, the kitten heard
leaves whispering in the trees.

Still the boy waited.
Still the kitten waited.

Inside, the boy heard
the tale of the Israelites leaving Egypt.

Outside, the kitten split
a twig in two.

Inside, the boy broke
the middle matzo in half.

Inside, the boy dipped
parsley into salt water.

Outside, the kitten chewed
a wet blade of grass.

Outside, the kitten
cleaned its paws.

Still the boy waited.
Still the kitten waited.

Inside, the boy
washed his hands.

Inside, the boy drank grape juice.
Outside, the kitten lapped at a puddle.

Author's Note

Passover, also known as the Festival of Freedom, is an eight-day Jewish holiday that celebrates the exodus of the enslaved Israelites from Egypt in approximately 1225 B.C.E. Passover occurs in the spring, beginning on the fifteenth day of the Jewish month of *Nisan*, which always falls on the night of the full moon.

The Israelites were not always enslaved in Egypt. They lived there peacefully for many years until a pharaoh who hated the Jews came into power and forced them into slavery.

According to the Book of Exodus, Moses was ordered by God to lead the Israelites out of Egypt. But the pharaoh would not let them go. After ten plagues befell the Egyptians (blood, frogs, vermin, wild beasts, pestilence, boils, hail, locusts, darkness, and the slaying of the firstborn), the pharaoh decided to let the Israelites leave.

Fearful that the pharaoh would change his mind, the Israelites fled in such a hurry that they did not even wait for their bread to rise. This is why during the eight days of Passover, Jewish families do not eat any bread or other foods made with leavening. Instead, we eat *matzo* (unleavened bread).

It is traditional for Jewish families to hold a special service at home called a *Seder* on the first two nights of Passover. "Seder" means order, and there are many steps to the Seder that take place in a particular order. Each person at the Seder takes turns reading from a book called a Haggadah, which serves as a guide to the Seder and tells the story of the Israelites' exodus from Egypt. During the evening, a festive meal is served.

After the festive meal is eaten and dessert, which includes the *afikomen*, is served, it is traditional to open the door for Elijah the Prophet. It is said that Elijah, who ascended to heaven in a fiery chariot, will return to earth to announce the coming of the Messiah and a time of peace. Each year we eagerly await Elijah and his hopeful message.

In many homes, it is customary for the children to open the door for Elijah. When I was growing up, Passover was my favorite holiday, and I especially loved to open the door for Elijah. I stood on the doorstep, feeling the cool night air on my face and gazing out into the darkness. I never caught a glimpse of Elijah, yet each year when I returned to the table, his cup was no longer full. Had Elijah actually come or had one of the grown-ups taken a few sips from his cup? It doesn't matter. What matters is that we all do what we can to help bring about a time of peace.

SOME TRADITIONAL RITUALS OF THE PASSOVER SEDER

lighting candles

drinking four cups of grape juice or wine

placing a cup filled with grape juice or wine on the table for Elijah the Prophet

washing hands

dipping spring greens into salt water

eating *matzo* (unleavened bread)

breaking the *afikomen* (the middle matzo) in two and hiding one piece of it

reciting the four questions, which ask "Why is this night different from all other nights?"

eating a festive meal

singing songs of praise

opening the door for Elijah the Prophet